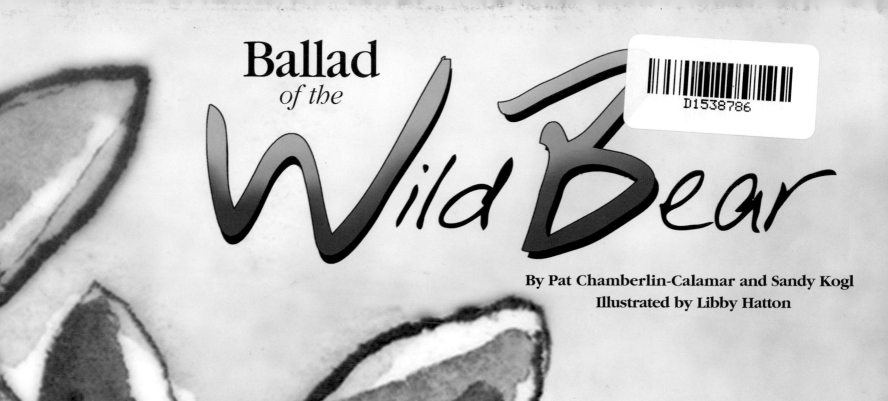

Ballad
of the
Wild Bear

By Pat Chamberlin-Calamar and Sandy Kogl
Illustrated by Libby Hatton

Alaska Natural History Association
Anchorage, Alaska

*For children everywhere—We hope you can experience and appreciate
wilderness and wild animals safely.*   —PCC, SK, and LH

Pat Chamberlin-Calamar has taught everything from music to English to guitar.
She and her husband, Don, have spent every summer in Alaska since 1985.
This is her second book for children.

Sandy Kogl has shared 40 years of her life with bears in Alaska, including
working as a park ranger at Denali National Park. She lives in Talkeetna
where she is a founding member of the Bear Necessities Coalition.

Libby Hatton has been living and hiking in Alaska's bear country, painting
Alaska's grandeur, and caring for Alaska's children (as Dr. Elizabeth Hatton,
Pediatrician) for more than 30 years.

Acknowledgements

The publisher would like to thank the following experts for their comments and
advice: John Hechtel and Colleen Matt with the Alaska Department of Fish and
Game, Terry DeBruyn with the National Park Service and John Schoen at Alaska
Audubon. The authors would like to thank: the Bear Necessities Coalition, Don
Calamar, Susan Chamberlin, David Kantz, Isaac Klotz, Liz Klotz-Chamberlin,
Peter Klotz-Chamberlin, Diane Calamar Okonek, Brian Okonek and Jim Okonek.

Text ©2003 Pat Chamberlin-Calamar and Sandy Kogl.
Illustrations ©2003 Libby Hatton.
Project Manager: Lisa Oakley
Editor: Jill Brubaker
Designed by: Chris Byrd

ISBN: 978-0-930931-88-1 (hardcover)

Library of Congress Cataloging-in-Publication Data
Chamberlin-Calamar, Pat.
Ballad of the wild bear / written by Pat Chamberlin-Calamar and Sandy Kogl ;
illustrated by Libby Hatton.
p. cm.
Summary: In this spin-off of the folk song "The Fox," bears and humans learn
how to live peacefully as neighbors.
ISBN 0-930931-61-0 (pbk. & cd)
1.   Children's songs, English-United States-Texts. [1. Bears-Songs and music.
2. Songs. 3. Human-animal relationships-Songs and music. 4. Alaska-Songs and
music. 5. Songs.] I. Kogl, Sandy. II. Hatton, Libby, ill. III. Title.

PZ8.3.C658 2004
782.42--dc22
2004006162

Alaska
Natural History
ASSOCIATION

750 West Second Avenue, Suite 100
Anchorage, Alaska 99501
www.alaskanha.org

A teaching guide to *Ballad of the Wild Bear*
is available by contacting the publisher.

A Note from the Publisher

Having bears as neighbors is a fact of life in Alaska, but it's not just Alaskans that must learn to be good neighbors to wild animals like bears. People across the country are increasingly becoming aware of the human impact on animal habitats and the difficulties of living side-by-side. The Alaska Natural History Association is pleased to be involved in bringing *Ballad of the Wild Bear* and its message to readers like you, young and old. In return for the privilege of publishing this work, the Association has set aside a fund for the Bear Necessities Coalition's Bear Aware Education Program.

Behind the Book

The summer of 2001 is well remembered in the small village of Talkeetna, Alaska. Grizzly and black bears had become accustomed to finding food in dumpsters and garbage cans, resulting in many unwelcome encounters with bears. Eventually six bears were shot. As a result of these conflicts, local residents launched a grassroots effort called The Bear Necessities Coalition with the goal of fostering human behavior that would help keep bears wild and people safe. This book evolved from the Coalition's desire to reach young people and create a lasting message that encourages bear conservation. Because of their commitment to keeping bears wild and people safe, the authors and the illustrator have contributed their work.

Grizzly prowled out on a chilly night,
Winked at the moon for shining so bright.
She had many a mile to go that night,
Before she reached the town-o, town-o, town-o.
She had many a mile to go that night,
Before she reached the town-o.

Her big brother went where people had been,
Found food careless folk had left out again.
Their picnic baskets were a treat for him,
He came back looking for more-o, more-o, more-o.
Their picnic baskets were a treat for him,
He came back looking for more-o.

Now that the boar liked the people's feast,
Something had to be done to stop this beast.
A bang was heard. His raid suddenly ceased.
He would never be free in the wild-o, wild-o, wild-o.
A bang was heard. His raid suddenly ceased.
He would never be free in the wild-o.

Will Grizzly's fate take a different twist?
Her trail to town is full of risk.
Can wild bears and people coexist?
Watch her hunting for food-o, food-o, food-o.
Can wild bears and people coexist?
Watch her hunting for food-o.

She ran until she came to a chicken shack,
Where the chicks did cluck and the ducks did quack.
The bear's big lips went smack, smack, smack,
But the fence bit her back in the nose-o, nose-o, nose-o.
The bear's big lips went smack, smack, smack,
But the fence bit her back in the nose-o.

Grizzly's hunger was bear size,
She went downtown for burgers and fries.
But sturdy garbage cans could not be pried,
She traveled on by for her meal-o, meal-o, meal-o.
But sturdy garbage cans could not be pried,
She traveled on by for her meal-o.

Where-o-where did the bird feeders hide?
Compost piles could not be tried.
Doggie treats were safe inside,
Grizz hurried off on the trail-o, trail-o, trail-o.
Doggie treats were safe inside,
Grizz hurried off on the trail-o.

She came to a camp that was clean as could be,
Cooking downwind was the key.
No food for Grizz to smell or see,
She ambled on by in the woods-o, woods-o, woods-o.
No food for Grizz to smell or see,
She ambled on by in the woods-o.

A family picking berries in the crisp fall air,
Came upon Grizz foraging for her winter fare.
They did not run. They were bear aware.
Knew how to stay safe from bears-o, bears-o, bears-o.
They did not run. They were bear aware.
Knew how to stay safe from bears-o.

Alaska's tundra turned purple, gold and red,
Grizz rummaged around for a snug dry bed.
With thick fur and fat belly for storms ahead,
She settled right down in her den-o, den-o, den-o.
With thick fur and fat belly for storms ahead,
She settled right down in her den-o.

Her baby cubs in the years to come,
The sow would teach them not to be troublesome.
Eat wild foods where they are from,
And never go near the town-o, town-o, town-o.
Eat wild foods where they are from,
And never go near the town-o.

Bear-aware folks can change people's minds,
To put away stuff where bears can't find.
If treated with respect by all humankind,
Bears will look for food in the wild-o, wild-o, wild-o.
If treated with respect by all humankind,
Bears will look for food in the wild-o.

So if you are hiking on a wilderness trail,
And you find some bear tracks, don't turn pale.
Just sing out loud and invent a tale,
About keeping bears wild in our world-o, world-o, world-o.
Just sing out loud and invent a tale,
About keeping bears wild in our world-o.

Glossary

Bear-Aware: knowing how to react if you encounter a bear.

Bear-Resistant Food Container (BRFC): a specially designed, lightweight, hard plastic container used to keep food and trash away from bears.

Boar: a mature male bear, usually 5-6 years old or older.

Compost: a mixture of kitchen and garden waste (leftover food, leaves, grass clippings) left in a pile or bin. As this material decomposes, a rich, organic matter is formed that can be used to enrich and improve soil quality.

Cooking Downwind: preparing all food so that the smells travel with the wind down, away from a campsite. By following this method, campers will not draw a bear into the camping area.

Cubs: a young grizzly bear, usually less than three years old. Cubs typically weigh less than a pound at birth, and 15 pounds when they emerge from their den in spring. They typically stay with their mother for two-and-a-half years.

Foraging: to hunt or search for food.

Habitat: region or area where a plant or animal is normally found. Grizzly bears live in a variety of habitats.

Hibernate: to spend the winter sleeping or resting.

Litter: a group of baby animals born at one time.

Sow: a mature female bear, usually 5-6 years old or older. She may produce a litter every three years. Litter size varies from 1 to 4, often averaging 2 cubs each time.

Sturdy Garbage Cans: heavy, metal garbage cans specially designed to prevent bears from getting inside.

Tundra: a treeless plain found in arctic regions where the ground beneath the surface is often frozen all year. Much of Alaska and northern Canada is tundra.

All About Grizzly Bears

What's In a Name?

The terms "grizzly bear" and "brown bear" are often used interchangeably for the species *Ursus arctos*. "Brown" bear is used to refer to all members of this species, though bears like those in our story that are found inland and in northern habitats are often called "grizzly" bears.

Grizzlies get their name from their coat which often has a light, silvery color, giving them a "grizzled" appearance. Fur color may vary from dark brown to light blond.

Where Do Grizzlies Live?

Grizzly bears live in a wide variety of habitats from alpine tundra to mixed forests to coastal beaches. Depending on how much food is available, their home range may be a few square miles or hundreds of square miles.

Approximately 32,000 grizzly bears live in Alaska where the population is stable and healthy. Only four other states have grizzlies left in the wild—Idaho, Montana, Washington and Wyoming—and their future is uncertain in these states. Thirteen states have declared grizzlies extinct. Canada grizzlies are stable in four provinces and extinct in two. While they once roamed in Mexico, they are now extinct there. Brown bears are abundant in Russia and occur in portions of Asia, including China and Japan, and also occur in smaller, fragmented populations in a number of European countries.

Grizzly Facts

Grizzly bears grow to seven to nine feet in length. Adult males, called boars, usually weigh between 500 and 1100 pounds. Females, called sows, are smaller and weigh 250 to 600 pounds.

A prominent shoulder hump and long, slightly curved claws are characteristic of grizzly bears. Grizzly bears have an excellent sense of smell, and their hearing and eyesight are similar to that of humans.

Grizzlies are omnivores, meaning they eat a variety of plant and animal foods. Common plant foods include roots, grasses and berries. Large mammals (moose, caribou, deer) and their young, small mammals (voles, ground squirrels), salmon, insect larvae and animal carcasses are among the common animal foods grizzlies like to eat.

Grizzly Bear

©Gary Lyon

When You Are in Bears' Home

Be Alert: Bears are active day and night. Watch for tracks and droppings. When hiking, stay together as a group and make noise to let bears know you are around (verses 9, 12).

Keep a Clean Camp: Choose a site with a good view of the area, store food and garbage properly, cook downwind and don't camp on a bear trail (verses 8, 12).

Never Approach a Bear: Give bears lots of space. If a bear is on the same trail you are on either go way around it, wait for it to move away, or choose a new direction (verses 9, 13).

Never Feed Bears: Don't leave food or garbage out where bears can find it. A bear that learns to look for human food may become aggressive toward people and eventually will get shot (verses 2, 3, 8, 12).

When Bears Live Next To Your Home

Bird Feeders: Only put them out in the winter when bears are most likely hibernating. Old seeds should be cleaned up each spring (verses 7, 12).

Electric Fences: Use them to protect farm animals, compost piles, beehives, and outdoor freezers from bears (verses 5, 7).

Fish Waste: Throw it into fast-moving water unless local regulations say otherwise (verse 8 illustration).

Garbage: Keep garbage in bear-proof cans and make regular trips to the dump in order to prevent smells that attract bears (verses 6, 12).

Human Food: Grills, picnics and snack foods should not be left out where bears can find them. Food and coolers should be stored inside a house or car (verses 2, 3, 12).

Pet Food: Keep it in a bear-proof container, a sturdy shed, garage, or in the house (verses 7, 12).

Problem Bears

"Problem Bears" are actually the result of "Problem People." Humans create the problem when they leave food out where bears can find it. Bears that have found food where people live and play will return again and again. If bears lose their fear of humans and continue to come looking for food, they present a potential danger to people.

Often the only way to deal with a problem bear is to destroy it, either by shooting it or giving it a deadly injection of poison. Preventing bears from finding human food is the best way to keep bears wild and people safe.

Educating people to respect bears and take simple steps to coexist with bears will help ensure future generations of people will have the opportunity to appreciate bears in the wild.

To Learn More

Alaska Department of Fish and Game
Wildlife Education Department
333 Raspberry Road, Anchorage, AK 99518
907-267-2168 or www.state.ak.us/adfg

Audubon Alaska
715 L Street, Suite 200, Anchorage, AK 99501
907-276-7034 or http://www.audubon.org/chapter/ak/ak/

Bear Necessities Coalition
P.O. Box 964
Talkeetna, AK 99676
907-733-2447 or E-mail: bearcoalition@gci.net